#1 Catacomb Mysteries©

Secret of the Catacombs

Mary Litton

To Jack, for the gift of time.

To Elizabeth, for the gift of a deadline.

www.CatacombMysteries.com

www.MaryLitton.com

Editor: Jack Bradford
Interior Director: Elizabeth Clare
ISBN-10: 0615615821
ISBN-13: 978-0615615820

CONTENTS

GETTING READY FOR THE SHOW

It was a cold fall morning at Saint John's Church. Will was dressed in his Sunday clothes – khaki pants and a blue button-down shirt that was too wrinkled, according to his mom, but they had not had time to iron it. His short brown hair was combed neatly to the side.

He kept his eyes on his third grade worksheet, his head bent over the Tiger Orange crayon, even though he *hated* to color. But even coloring was better than joining the other kids, who were practicing for the talent show.

Will rolled his eyes as he thought about it. Saint John's youth group was putting on a talent show to raise money for new playground equipment. Most of the kids had eagerly signed up to perform, but Will could not think of anything exciting about it, so he sat quietly in his seat, hoping nobody would notice.

He reached for the crayon basket and quickly glanced across the table. The only other kid still sitting there was Hannah, and she was coloring just as hard as he was. She stole a glance at him, too, and then they both quickly looked away.

Will turned to look at the other kids, laughing and goofing off. Anna, Sarah, and Jessica were working on a song and dance routine. The Terrible Thompson Twins were practicing a karate demonstration. And even the very serious

Aiden had decided to partner with Beth for a piano duet.

Will looked back at Hannah, his cheeks turning warm and his belly getting a little flip-floppy.

Then something large and blue caught Will's attention. He breathed in sharply as he saw his short, stout third-grade religious education teacher, Mrs. Smotherly, waddling in their direction. He bent down over his paper even more and felt his face get redder and hotter, wishing she would turn away.

Suddenly, she was in front of him, peering down at him through her thick black-rimmed glasses that magnified her eyes so much that they looked too big for her head. She pressed her bright orange lips together and shook her puff of cloud-like white hair.

"Do you need me to help you think of an act, dearie?" she asked. Will caught a whiff of peppermint candy on her breath.

He opened his mouth to protest when suddenly, the door to the classroom swung open and Father Dan walked in. Will felt a rush of relief.

"Just checking in on my talent show stars," Father Dan announced, looking around the room at the different acts. He then turned to see Will and Hannah, still coloring. Will felt embarrassed and slumped even closer to the paper, pretending to concentrate. He hoped Father Dan would not say anything to him in front of everyone.

"Excellent work, Will and Hannah," he said, admiring their drawings before walking around the room to inspect the others at work.

When he finished watching all the acts and sent the Terrible Thompson Twins to their separate corners, he turned back toward Will's table. "Does anyone have a minute to help me out with the set?"

Will shot his hand up so fast that he flew out of his chair and knocked it backwards, making the other kids giggle.

Father Dan pretended not to notice as he unfolded a piece of paper and handed it to him. "I need you to go down to the storage room and find the backdrop for the stage. It's in Room 3C, right here on the map." He pointed to a room that looked like it was in the middle of a giant maze. Will noticed that the room was on a floor called "the Catacombs."

"What does 'the Catacombs' level mean?" he asked.

Father Dan smiled and said, "Catacombs are old, underground passageways that churches built a very long time ago. Many were used as cemeteries or secret ways to get in and out of the church. We just use ours as the basement for storage."

Will swallowed hard. "So, nobody is buried down there, right?"

Father Dan shook his head. "Not unless we forgot someone."

Will gasped, but Father Dan just laughed. "I'm only kidding. We just keep our sets and decorations down there. Now, do you think you can find the backdrop for me?"

Will's heart beat fast in his chest, but he did not want to let Father Dan down. "No problem, I can do it," he replied.

"Oh, and you'll need this," Father Dan said, pulling out a long, black flashlight that looked like it belonged to a night watchman.

"Oh," Will said, his eyes growing big. "Is it dark down there?"

"There's no electricity in the hallways," Father Dan replied, then clapped Will on the back. "You'll be fine."

Will nodded. He tried to agree, but his mouth felt too dry to speak.

2

FINDING A FRIEND

Will studied the map as he walked out into the hallway.

"Hey, Will!" he heard someone say. He looked up and saw his neighbor Molly sitting outside her second-grade classroom. Molly looked very colorful in a bright purple dress, blue striped tights, and pink snow boots. A headband adorned with a large purple butterfly held her straight blonde hair back from her face. "Where are you going?" she asked.

"I'm getting the set for the talent show," he said, showing her the map and the flashlight.

"Cool!" Molly said, jumping up beside him and pointing at the map. "Is that where you're going?"

"Yeah, it's called the Catacombs, but it's really just the basement," Will said. "It used to be a cemetery," he added, feeling proud that he was assigned to this adventure.

"Can I come with you?" Molly asked, bouncing up and down in her boots.

"Aren't you supposed to be in class?" he asked.

"I got in trouble," she said, looking sheepishly at the floor. "Come on, let me go with you! They won't even know I'm gone! And I can't possibly get into any more trouble than I'm already in!"

Will shrugged. He didn't want to get in trouble for taking Molly along, but he realized he wanted someone to go with him. "Okay, but let's make it fast."

Molly squealed and clapped. "We're going on an adventure!" She grabbed the flashlight from Will and turned it up against her chin so that it lit up her face. "To the dark catacombs," she said with a scary laugh.

Will grabbed the flashlight and shoved it in his pocket. "Let's just go get the set and get back to class."

3

SECRETS IN THE CATACOMBS

"Wow, it's dark down here," whispered Molly, stepping a little closer to Will as he fumbled to turn on the flashlight. Their eyes adjusted to the dark as they watched the circular beam of light run along the cement walls of the long hallway in front of them.

Molly breathed in deeply. "It smells kind of funky down here."

Will shivered. "Here, you take the flashlight while I pull out the map," he said, handing the light to Molly. As he took the map out of his pocket and began to unfold it, the light and Molly suddenly vanished.

Will inhaled sharply. "Molly!" he cried out.

There was no answer. Will began to breathe hard as he turned around in a circle, trying to see in front of him. He felt lost and could not remember which way was forwards or backwards. "Molly!" he yelled again.

Suddenly, he saw a bright light.

"BOO!" screamed Molly, shining the light directly in his eyes. Will jumped into the air with fright as Molly doubled over with laughter. "Gotcha!" she giggled.

Will was so mad that he couldn't speak. He jerked the flashlight out of Molly's hand.

"Sheesh, it was a joke," Molly said. Will ignored her and studied the map in his trembling hands. He wanted to get out of there as fast as possible.

He took a minute to memorize the twists and turns of the different hallways, and then folded the map and put it back into his pocket.

"Hey, wait up!" Molly cried, sounding a little nervous as he disappeared into the tunnel.

They wound their way through the twists and turns until Will suddenly stopped. "It should be right around here," he said, shining the light on the wall and feeling with his hand.

"Over here," Molly cried. Will illuminated the wall in front of her and saw her pointing at a small handle. Together they pushed on the wall, and it swung open like a hidden door.

Will quickly scanned the light beam around the pitch-black room and saw a long chain connected to a single light bulb hanging from the ceiling.

He focused the flashlight on the chain and whispered to Molly, "Go pull that."

She hesitated as she tried to see in the darkness. Quietly, she tiptoed over and pulled the string. A bright yellow bulb lit up the room.

"AAAAH!" they both screamed and jumped toward the door.

There was a woman standing in the corner.

"Don't be scared," the woman said in a soothing voice. She was dressed in tan pants and a white button-down shirt. Her dark curly hair was pulled back into a ponytail, and she had eyes as warm as chocolate. She smiled and reached out her hands to welcome them. "I've been waiting for you, Will and Molly."

"How did you know our names?" Will asked over his shoulder. He was already facing the other way, prepared to run.

"I was sent to help you," the woman said.

"But if Father Dan knew you were down here, why did he send me?" Will asked.

"He wasn't the one who sent me." She took a step forward. "My name is Angie. God sent me to ask for your help."

"God sent you?" Will said, taking a step backward toward the door.

"He asked for *my* help?" Molly asked, thinking she had misheard.

"Yes," Angie nodded to both of them.

Will and Molly looked at each other and then back at Angie. "Why would He need our help?"

"Hang on," Angie said, and then held a finger up to her ear. Will noticed that she was wearing a small black earpiece like the one his father wore when he was talking on the phone.

"Yes, Sir, they're here," she said to the invisible person on the other line. She listened and smiled. "Very surprised, Sir. I'm giving them the mission now."

She turned back toward Will and Molly. "Molly, He says that He was really proud of that goal you scored in the game last week."

Molly gasped. She had been so happy last week when she had scored the winning goal for her soccer team.

Angie turned to Will. "And He said that all you need to say is, 'Hannah, do you want to be my partner for the talent show?' and she will say yes. She also has a great idea for an act; she's just too shy to ask anyone to do it with her."

Will's mouth dropped open. He knew it was God.

"Are you an angel?" Molly asked.

Angie smiled and nodded.

"But you don't look like an angel," Will said. "Where's your halo and the harp and the white robe?"

Angie laughed. "We like to blend in whenever we come here. We're everywhere, all the time; you just can't pick us out."

"But why would you need a phone to talk to God?" Molly asked, looking at the earpiece.

"Oh, I don't need this," Angie smiled. "I just love playing with all of your fun gadgets. You humans are so clever. Technology and bubble gum, my two favorite things down here." She suddenly chomped on a piece of gum they had not noticed before.

"What does God need from us?" Molly asked.

A frown quickly replaced Angie's smile. "Something bad is happening. Someone has found our secret time portal."

"There really is a time portal?" Will asked with excitement. He was a big fan of time travel books, where characters find secret doors that send them back in history to see things like dinosaurs or the Revolutionary War.

"Yes, and someone is using it for bad things. They are going back to biblical times and trying to change things."

"If they are changing history, then that means things will be different today," Will said. He knew from these books that the characters had to be really careful, because the slightest change in the past could rewrite history.

"Exactly," said Angie. "They are changing the Bible stories. We need your help to go back and fix things before the history of Christianity is altered."

Molly shook her head. "How can we go back into history?"

Angie cupped her hands together, closed her eyes, and mumbled something. Then she slowly opened her hands to reveal two shiny gold crosses that looked like something that would fit on a necklace. The gold was so shiny that it hurt Will and Molly's eyes.

"Take one, each of you," Angie said. The cross felt warm to Will; suddenly, he did not feel afraid. Molly smiled as she stroked the pretty design on her cross.

Angie walked over to the pull chain attached to the light. "This chain will pull you back in time."

"You mean, the time portal is a light that people use?" Will asked.

Angie smiled and nodded. "Sometimes the best hiding spots are right out in the open."

Molly shook her head. "That never works in hide and seek," she mumbled, thinking of her three-year-old brother, who always ruined the game by hiding in plain sight.

"Why didn't we go back in time when Molly pulled it?"

"Not anyone who pulls the chain goes back in time. Only the two who hold the gold crosses and pull the chain together can go back in time."

"How do we know which Bible story to go to?" Molly asked.

"I will give you the Bible verse that will take you to the right story. When you pull the chain, you have to say the verse. Once you get there, God will provide you with what you need, but you must fix the problem before it becomes too late."

Will stepped forward with his cross and grabbed the chain. "Can you tell us where we're going?"

Angie shook her head. "You will know only when you arrive."

"What problem are we fixing?" asked Molly.

"You'll have to figure that out when you get there," Angie replied.

"What if we can't figure it out?" Molly and Will asked together.

Angie smiled warmly. "Have you been paying attention in church?"

They both nodded.

"Then you will know what needs to be fixed."

Molly stood back, holding the glowing cross. She looked like she might cry.

"What's wrong, Molly?" Will asked.

Molly sniffled. "It's just that I think God has the wrong Molly. I'm always getting into trouble," she said quietly, looking at the floor.

"He knows exactly which Molly you are," Angie said. "Just because you can't sit still during the lessons and you sometimes forget the rules does not mean you are a bad person. God loves your energy. He needs someone with your brave spirit and sense of adventure."

Molly looked up at Angie with hope in her eyes.

Angie continued, "God gave you a feisty spirit to be used for something important, like saving the world!"

This did make sense to Molly. She never meant to get into trouble, but she always felt like doing much more than coloring and sitting in chairs, learning lessons that way. Molly gripped her cross in one hand and walked over to grab the chain with the other.

Angie nodded. "To go back in time, you must repeat this verse together. Isaiah 41:13 'For I the LORD your God will hold your right hand, saying to you, Fear not; I will help you.'"

They looked at Angie. "Aren't you coming with us?" Will asked, ready to pull the string.

"I can't come with you. But God will be looking out for you and give you what you need to get the job done."

Molly's eyes grew larger. "You mean, like secret spy gadgets?"

Angie smiled. "Something like that. Now you must go!"

Molly took a deep breath and turned to Will. Together they repeated, "'For I the LORD your God will hold your right hand, saying to you, Fear not; I will help you.'"

4

WILD ANIMALS

When they pulled the string, the bulb released an intense, white light brighter than the sun. The room was flooded with light, causing Molly and Will to hide their eyes in the crooks of their elbows. They gripped the chain tightly as a great wind swirled around them. The wind became so strong that they felt themselves lifting off the ground with a loud whoosh. Will felt his stomach drop like he was on a roller coaster. Molly tried to scream, but nothing came out.

Suddenly everything went dark and still. Molly's feet were back on the floor, and Will felt something wet drop on his arm and then on his face. He removed his hands from his eyes and realized that what he felt was rain. He was standing under a grove of palm trees, their leaves providing protection from the falling rain!

He and Molly turned around in circles, looking at the beauty of the large palm fronds. The steady sound of rain on the leaves mixed with the unusual sounds of exotic birds and animals.

"What just happened?" Molly asked. She noticed that the pull chain was gone and that her hand was clutching nothing but air.

Will looked down at his body to make sure everything was in order. He looked perfectly normal. "I think we just traveled through time," he grinned.

"That was awesome!" Molly laughed.

Will suddenly noticed something bulging in his pocket. He reached in and pulled out a metal can with a red horn attached to the lid. "What is this?" he asked.

Molly recognized it instantly. "Oh, it's an air horn! They use them at my soccer games and at field day." She took the can from Will. "You just do this!" She pushed down on the top and a loud, shrill "WAAAAAAAA!!!!" erupted, making Will nearly jump out of his skin.

He grabbed the can from her to make the horrible noise stop. His ears rang and his pulse raced. "Do *not* do that again!" he warned. Once it was safely back in his pocket, he looked around. "Why do you think I have an air horn?"

Molly gasped. "It's a spy tool!" She began patting her pockets and then she smiled as she reached into one. She pulled out a fistful of baby carrots, and her face fell into a frown. "What are these?"

Will laughed. "Did you forget to eat your vegetables today?"

"Very funny," Molly huffed, clearly upset by the choice of her spy gear. "Maybe they're secret weapons disguised as carrots," she said. She launched one into the air, covering her ears in case it exploded. It landed back in the tall grass with the soft *thud,* like a normal carrot.

Will rolled his eyes and began to look around. He thought he heard voices, and when he looked through the tree branches, he saw something large and wooden. "Come on," he said, heading toward the sounds.

Molly followed while studying her carrots, trying to find a secret use for them. "Maybe there's a hidden laser, and if I can just find the switch. . ."

"Shhhh!!" Will suddenly hushed her.

She looked up and stopped in her tracks.

They realized they were standing at the back of a wooden structure as large as a three-story building. It was long and rectangular, with three decks. There were two gray trunks sticking out of one window and a pair of spotted necks sticking out of another window.

"Elephants? Giraffes?" Molly asked.

Will's eyes grew wide as he realized where they were. This was not a building. This was a boat!

"It's the ark!" Will exclaimed. "This is Noah's ark!"

They looked in awe at the massive ship built of cypress wood. "Look at all the animals," Molly whispered.

hought carefully. "The ark was ...d 450 feet long; that's longer than a football field. It was one of the biggest and best-designed ships in history."

"That's because God gave Noah the exact design," Molly replied. "Remember the story? He saw that the world was full of evil and sin, so he wanted to flood the earth and start over. But he saw that Noah and his family were good. So he told Noah of his plans to flood the earth and gave him exact instructions for building the ark."

Will was still thinking hard. "God gave him the perfect ratio of its massive height and weight, so it would be stable on water.

"Can you imagine what people must have said about him? 'This is so weird, a huge boat in the middle of a field!' They must have made fun of him!"

Will nodded, realizing for the first time how brave Noah must have been. He was sure that his friends had probably laughed at him and called him names, too, sometimes. "I'm not sure I would have had the guts to keep building it if everyone else is making fun of me."

"Also, God sent a male and female of each animal so that they could have babies and repopulate the earth after the flood," Molly said. "That could not have been easy – I mean, to figure out how to get them all on this boat."

Will looked up at the sky. "Wait, and the rain! God made it rain for forty days and forty nights. That must mean the flood is coming soon!"

Just then, two men in robes came running down the wooden ramp toward the grassy marsh where they were standing. Will and Molly had no time to hide as the men approached them.

"Who are you?" the younger man asked.

Molly held up her hands like Angela and said in a weird sing-songy voice, "Do not be afraid. We come in peace."

Will rolled his eyes and elbowed Molly. "God sent us to help you," he said in a normal voice.

"You must be Noah," Molly said, staring at him with a funny grin. She felt a little star-struck.

"Yes," Noah answered. "I'm glad He sent you. We don't know how they got out."

"I checked their stall this morning, and there were two of them," the younger man said. "And I just noticed the stall door was open, and now they're gone."

"You lost some animals?" Will asked.

"It must be the unicorns!" Molly gasped. She knew the legend had to be true!

"The horses," the young man replied. "The horses are gone."

"We don't have time to look," Noah said. "It's raining much harder. The flood will be here any minute."

"You can't leave the horses," Molly said. "If they don't get on the boat, then all of the horses will be killed."

"The flood is going to come soon; we don't have time to go find them," Noah said sadly.

"We'll go look for them," Molly offered. "God sent us to help you. He must have sent us to look for the horses."

"Do what you can," Noah said. "But you must hurry."

He and the younger man turned and walked quickly back toward the ramp.

Will looked at Molly. His heart was racing. "How are we going to find the horses in time?"

"Remember the verse, Will. 'For I the LORD your God will hold your right hand, saying to you, Fear not; I will help you.'" Molly said. "God will help us figure out something. I can't imagine life without horses."

"Where do you think they went?" Will asked.

The rain was coming down so hard that Molly had to cover her head with her arms. "I know if I were a horse, I'd try to get out of this rain!"

"That's it!" Will shouted. He grabbed Molly's hand and took off, running for the trees. "Let's go find the horses!"

5

LOOKING FOR HORSES

Will and Molly huddled under a palm tree on the edge of the small forest, shivering from the rain. "I don't see anything," Will said, scanning the tree line.

"Will," Molly said, her voice a trembling whisper.

Will glanced at Molly and saw that her eyes were big with fear. He looked over toward the grassy marsh and froze in his tracks.

Not more than two hundred feet away and staring right at them was a very large, striped orange tiger.

Will could not help but notice that it was the very same color as his crayon.

The tiger twitched its tail and opened its jaws, exposing a set of deadly sharp fangs, and let out a deafening roar.

Molly gasped and grabbed Will's hand. Will felt like he was going to get sick, but suddenly he had an idea.

He slowly reached into his pocket and pulled out the air horn.

"Good idea," Molly whispered as she covered her ears.

Will knew that this was either a really good idea, or it would be the end of them if the tiger decided to attack. He had to trust that God had given him the can for a reason.

He took a deep breath and pushed down as hard as he could. The sharp "WAAAAAAAA" blasted from the can in the tiger's direction.

The tiger roared with anger and then turned around and ran. It sprinted far away in the opposite direction.

Molly jumped up and cheered. "You did it, Will! You saved us!"

Will grinned, "I know!" he said. "I did it!"

"Let's go," Molly said, pulling him back toward the sparse forest of trees. "We have to save the horses!"

6

WALKING THROUGH WATER

Back in the forest, Will looked for any signs of horses.

"Will," Molly shouted over the pounding rain. "Over there!"

She pointed toward a large group of trees where something black and hairy was twitching.

It was a tail.

They ran toward the trees and saw two small brown horses with black manes and tails chewing on the grass. As they got closer, the horses startled and began running for the next grove of trees.

"Oh, no, they're afraid of us!" Will shouted. "What can we do?"

"I know!" Molly said. She ran over to one of the trees and began to climb up the limbs. "Come on!"

Will hesitated. He looked up. He had never been good at climbing trees, and now with the rain, he was scared.

"Come on," Molly said. "You can do it!"

Will put his foot on the trunk and tried to pull himself up, but he slipped and crashed back to the soggy ground.

A loud clap of thunder boomed in the sky.

"Hurry!" Molly shouted.

Will stood up. He took a breath, closed his eyes, and said a quick prayer. *God, please help me.*

He opened his eyes and put his foot back on the trunk, grabbed a low branch with his hands, and pulled himself up. He suddenly felt much stronger and braver than he had ever felt. Quickly, he found himself hugging the same branch as Molly.

"Now what?" he asked, holding on to the branch tightly.

Molly smiled and pulled the carrots out of her pocket. She threw one in the horse's direction. The horse looked at it and then trotted over to eat it. When it finished, Molly dropped another carrot right under her. "When it comes over to eat it, you have to jump on its back!" she whispered to Will.

"What?!" Will asked. Climbing a tree was one thing, but jumping onto a horse's back was completely different.

"That's the only way! We have to ride them back to the ark!" Molly exclaimed, just as the horse came for the carrot.

"Remember the verse," she yelled.

Will closed his eyes and together they shouted, "'Fear not; I will help you!'"

"Now!" Molly whispered, hitting Will in the ribs so hard that he lost his grip and began to fall.

"Aah!" he yelled, tumbling out of the tree and landing on top of the surprised horse. He squeezed its neck with all his might.

"Use its mane!" Molly yelled from the tree.

Will grabbed fistfuls of the horse's mane just as Molly lured the second horse over and dropped down on top of it, too. The horses began to gallop in circles.

Then Molly threw carrots in the direction of the ark, and both horses began to settle down.

Soon, the horses were calmly following Molly's trail of carrots back toward the marsh. They came out of the forest and could see the ark's ramp still down across the marsh.

"The boat's still open!" Molly called.

Suddenly, Molly's horse whinnied and bucked up. "Whoa!" Molly yelled, grabbing the horse's neck so she would not fall off.

"What's wrong?" Will asked as his horse began to turn around in a circle and stamp its foot.

"Something has spooked them," Molly said, trying to soothe her horse.

Will scanned the marsh. "Is the tiger back?" He did not see any sign of the tiger or any other animal. But then he noticed that he could barely see the tall grass. It was covered in water.

The marsh was starting to flood.

"Hey!" Will shouted. "The marsh is flooding!"

"We have to get to that boat before it's too late!" Molly said.

"I thought horses could swim," Will said, petting his horse's neck to calm it down.

"I read about this in one of my books. They can swim, but if they haven't done it before, they can be nervous."

"Then what do we do?" Will asked.

Molly flipped onto her belly and slid off her horse, landing in a big puddle. "We have to lead them."

Will looked at the ground far below him and swallowed hard.

"Jump down!" Molly said. She held out a carrot far enough away to make the horse take a few steps forward in the water.

Will flipped onto his stomach and tried to slide off gracefully like Molly, but he fell backward and hit the wet ground with a large WHUMP.

"Smooth move," Molly laughed as she helped him up. Will wiped the mud on his pants and then took a few carrots from Molly.

"This reminds me of my dog's obedience class," Will said, dangling a carrot in his hand so that the horse could see it, but could not eat it.

They began to lead the horses through the marsh, the water getting deeper and deeper as they got closer to the ark.

Soon, the water was up to their hips, making it hard to walk. Their legs were so tired, they began to shake.

Will squinted through the rain at the ark. Even though they were close, it seemed impossibly far away. He was not sure he could keep going.

"Hey!" Molly suddenly yelled. "Hey! Down here!" She began waving her hands frantically. Will looked up and saw Noah and the other man looking down at them from the deck.

"Hey!" Will shouted, jumping up and down and waving his arms. He had a sudden burst of energy. "Help!" he cried.

The men disappeared inside the boat. Will glanced at Molly, who looked like she might cry. "I don't think we're going to make it," she sniffed.

Just then, the men appeared at the top of the ramp. Then, several other men and women joined them and ran down the ramp, wading through the water toward them.

"You found them!" Noah said, taking Molly's horse so she could walk.

"Just in time," the younger man said, pushing Will's horse from behind.

"Who are these people?" Molly asked as two women helped pull her up to the ramp.

"My family," Noah smiled proudly.

Will nodded. "They are good people. I'm glad God chose you."

7

THE FLOOD IS COMING

Once they were back on the ark, Will and Molly offered to take the horses back to the stall while Noah and his family checked on the rest of the animals.

They walked past stalls filled with two of every kind of animal. There were all sorts of strange sounds and smells. It was like visiting a private indoor zoo!

They led the horses into the last empty stall.

"That was my first time on a horse," Will said, patting his horse's snout. The horse nuzzled up to Will's cheek like it was giving him a kiss. "Hey," Will laughed, pushing it away, "cut it out!"

"You know what would help Noah keep track of all of his animals?" Molly asked.

"What?"

"A cow-culator," she laughed. Will rolled his eyes and shook his head.

They walked over to one of the boat's decks and looked out at the flooding marsh. "Do you think the world will ever flood again?" Molly asked.

"Remember how God made the rainbow as a promise that he would never flood the earth again?" Will said.

"That's right," Molly said. "That's why we see a rainbow every time it rains."

Just then, they heard a large rumbling
sound and the ground began to shake.
They looked out and saw a huge wall of
water heading through the forest,
knocking trees down like a gigantic lawn
mower. The roaring sound of rushing
water was almost deafening.

The flood was here.

As the waves came crashing toward the boat, they screamed and grabbed on to each other. Just as the water was about to hit the boat, they closed their eyes, and everything went dark and still.

8

BACK HOME

Everything was strangely quiet. Molly opened one eye and saw that they were no longer standing on the ark about to be hit by water. Instead, they were back in the basement room of their church. The pull chain hung above them, perfectly still as if it had not been touched.

She and Will looked at each other, embarrassed to still be hugging, and quickly stepped apart.

"That was so scary!" Molly said, still shaking. "Watching the earth flood must have been really frightening for Noah and his family."

"You did it!" Angie clapped. "You saved the horses!"

"Yeah, we did!" Molly said, twirling and taking a bow.

"Who let the horses out?" Will asked.

"Do you think they'll do it again?" Molly asked.

"God asked for you two to find out and stop it if it happens again." She picked up a large backdrop and handed it out to Will. "Don't forget what you came down here for."

"Oh, yeah," Will said. He had forgotten all about the talent show.

"You better go quickly before anyone notices that you're missing."

Will and Molly started to leave, but Will wanted to ask one more question.

When he turned around, Angie was no longer there.

He turned to Molly. Her eyes were huge. "That really happened, right?" he asked. Molly nodded and said, "Yes."

9

BACK TO CLASS

Back on the top floor, Will stopped outside Molly's Sunday school classroom.

"That was really fun. Thanks for letting me come along," Molly said.

"Sure," Will said. "You were really good with those secret spy carrots."

Molly laughed. "You were really brave, Will."

Will blushed and looked away. He felt proud. "You, too. See you next week."

Will walked back in his classroom. "There you are!" Father Dan said, walking over to get the backdrop. "Did you have any trouble finding the place?"

"No trouble at all," Will said.

Father Dan scrunched up his eyebrows and looked at Will. "Is your hair wet?"

Will ran his hand through his wet hair and shrugged. He walked back to his table, where Hannah was still coloring. "Hey, Hannah, want to be my partner for the talent show?"

Hannah looked up and smiled. "Sure, Will! I was hoping you would ask me. I have a great idea for an act!"

Genesis 6:13 – 8:22 NRSV

And God said to Noah, 'I have determined to make an end of all flesh, for the earth is filled with violence because of them; now I am going to destroy them along with the earth. Make yourself an ark of cypress wood; make rooms in the ark, and cover it inside and out with pitch. This is how you are to make it: the length of the ark three hundred cubits, its width fifty cubits, and its height thirty cubits. Make a roof for the ark, and finish it to a cubit above; and put the door of the ark in its side; make it with lower, second, and third decks. For my part, I am going to bring a flood of waters on the earth, to destroy from under heaven all flesh in which is the breath of life; everything that is on the earth shall die. But I will establish my covenant with you; and you shall come into the ark, you, your sons, your wife, and your sons' wives with you. And of every living thing, of all flesh, you shall bring two of every kind into the ark, to keep them alive with you; they shall be male and female. Of the birds according to their kinds, and of the animals according to their kinds, of every creeping thing of the ground according to its kind, two of every kind shall come in to you, to keep them alive. Also take with you every kind of food that is eaten, and store it up; and it shall serve as food for you and for them.' Noah did this; he did all that God commanded him.

Genesis 7

Then the Lord said to Noah, 'Go into the ark, you and all your household, for I have seen that you alone are righteous before me in this generation. Take with you seven pairs of all clean animals, the male and its mate; and a pair of the animals that are not clean, the male and its mate; and seven pairs of the birds of the air also, male and female, to keep their kind alive on the face of all the earth. For in seven days I will send rain on the earth for forty days and forty nights; and every living thing that I have made I will blot out from the face of the ground.' And Noah did all that the Lord had commanded him.

Noah was six hundred years old when the flood of waters came on the earth. And Noah with his sons and his wife and his sons' wives went into the ark to escape the waters of the flood. Of clean animals, and of animals that are not clean, and of birds, and of everything that creeps on the ground, two and two, male and female, went into the ark with Noah, as God had commanded Noah. And after seven days the waters of the flood came on the earth.

In the six-hundredth year of Noah's life, in the second month, on the seventeenth day of the month, on that day all the fountains of the great deep burst forth, and the windows of the heavens were opened. The rain fell on the earth for forty days and forty nights. On the very same day Noah with his sons, Shem and Ham and Japheth, and Noah's wife and the three wives of his sons, entered the ark, they and every wild animal of every kind, and all domestic animals of every kind, and every creeping thing that creeps on the earth, and every bird of every kind—every bird, every winged creature. They went into the ark with Noah, two and two of all flesh in which there was the breath of life. And those that entered, male and female of all flesh, went in as God had commanded him; and the Lord shut him in.

 The flood continued for forty days on the earth; and the waters increased, and bore up the ark, and it rose high above the earth. The waters swelled and increased greatly on the earth; and the ark floated on the face of the waters. The waters swelled so mightily on the earth that all the high mountains under the whole heaven were covered; the waters swelled above the mountains, covering them fifteen cubits deep. And all flesh died that moved on the earth, birds, domestic animals, wild animals, all swarming creatures that swarm on the earth, and all human beings; everything on dry land in whose nostrils was the breath of life died. He blotted out every living thing that was on the face of the ground, human beings and animals and creeping things and birds of the air; they were blotted out from the earth. Only Noah was left, and those that were with him in the ark. And the waters swelled on the earth for one hundred and fifty days.

Genesis 8

But God remembered Noah and all the wild animals and all the domestic animals that were with him in the ark. And God made a wind blow over the earth, and the waters subsided; the fountains of the deep and the windows of the heavens were closed, the rain from the heavens was restrained, and the waters gradually receded from the earth. At the end of one hundred and fifty days the waters had abated; and in the seventh month, on the seventeenth day of the month, the ark came to rest on the mountains of Ararat. The waters continued to abate until the tenth month; in the tenth month, on the first day of the month, the tops of the mountains appeared.

At the end of forty days Noah opened the window of the ark that he had made and sent out the raven; and it went to and fro until the waters were dried up from the earth. Then he sent out the dove from him, to see if the waters had subsided from the face of the ground; but the dove found no place to set its foot, and it returned to him to the ark, for the waters were still on the face of the whole earth. So he put out his hand and took it and brought it into the ark with him. He waited another seven days, and again he sent out the dove from the ark; and the dove came back to him in the evening, and there in its beak was a freshly plucked olive leaf; so Noah knew that the waters had subsided from the earth. Then he waited another seven days, and sent out the dove; and it did not return to him any more.

In the six hundred and first year, in the first month, on the first day of the month, the waters were dried up from the earth; and Noah removed the covering of the ark, and looked, and saw that the face of the ground was drying. In the second month, on the twenty-seventh day of the month, the earth was dry. Then God said to Noah, 'Go out of the ark, you and your wife, and your sons and your sons' wives with you. Bring out with you every living thing that is with you of all flesh—birds and animals and every creeping thing that creeps on the earth—so that they may abound on the earth, and be fruitful and multiply on the earth.' So Noah went out with his sons and his wife and his sons' wives. And every animal, every creeping thing, and every bird, everything that moves on the earth, went out of the ark by families.

Then Noah built an altar to the Lord, and took of every clean animal and of every clean bird, and offered burnt-offerings on the altar. And when the Lord smelt the pleasing odor, the Lord said in his heart,

'I will never again curse the ground because of humankind, for the inclination of the human heart is evil from youth; nor will I ever again destroy every living creature as I have done. As long as the earth endures,seedtime and harvest, cold and heat summer and winter, day and night shall not cease.'

ACKNOWLEDGMENTS

I would like to thank all of my wonderful family and friends who have supported my writing over the years and told me not to give up on my dreams. Thank you to Art and Jenny for encouraging me to always think big. Thank you to Mary and James for always having your typewriter available. Thank you to Jennie, Erin, Book Club, the Wades, the Penberthys, and the rest of my early readers for your suggestions, ideas and encouragement. Thank you to Amie for all of your emotional and logistical support. Finally, thank you to David for the unconditional love and support you have given me, and for being brave enough to tell me that I would be miserable making sandwiches.

DON'T MISS WILL AND MOLLY'S NEXT
CATACOMBS MYSTERIES© ADVENTURE!

#1 Secret of the Catacombs

#2 The Vanishing Act

#3 Beginning of the End

To learn more about The Catacombs Mysteries© series
and order your next book, visit the series web site:

www.CatacombMysteries.com